COPYRIGHT © 1999 The Wordhouse Pty. Ltd. Melbourne, Australia.

Art direction: Jeff Piatkowski, Melbourne.
Film: Colour Image Makers, Melbourne.
Published by The Wordhouse Pty Ltd, Melbourne, Australia.

National Library of Australia Cataloguing in Publication entry:

Merry, Paul, 1949-

Teddy Cool Cleans Up.

ISBN 0-646-35991-6

I. Coutts, Lisa. II. Title.

A823.3

TEDDY COOL CLEANS UP

Story by Paul Merry
Illustrations by Lisa Coutts

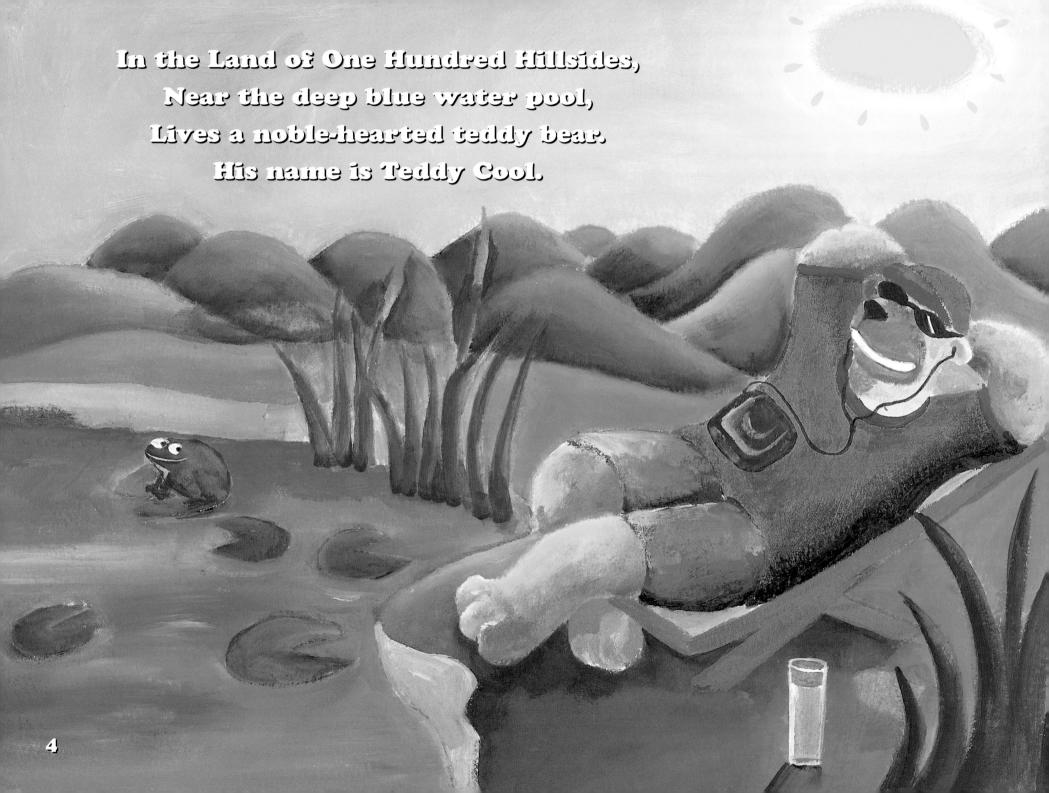

In the Land of One Hundred Hillsides,
Near the deep blue water pool,
Lives a noble-hearted teddy bear.
His name is Teddy Cool.

Teddy Cool's as cool as cool can be.
He's brave, he's strong and true,
And when a problem bothers him,
He coolly thinks it through.

Today a soap mine's on his mind.
They're mining near his home.
They're digging up the countryside.
They're filling it with foam.

6

The rabbits, moles and wombats come
With barrows, spades and picks.
They bring the soap out from the mine
In baskets made from sticks.

They cut it into soapy chunks.
Then they hose it down.
They load it onto noisy trucks,
Which take the soap to town.

Now the Land of One Hundred Hillsides
Is noisy all the time,
Its crystal pools made soapy,
All spoiled by the mine.

9

With ugly holes dug in the hills
And waste for all to see,
The locals find their peaceful life
Is a wistful memory.

10

The buffaloes are snorting mad.
They're almost having fits.
They want to charge into the mine
And smash the place to bits.

"This calls for calm," cried Katy Owl.
"It calls for coolness too.
It calls for thinking things right through.
It calls for you know who-ooo-ooo."

12

So they call on Teddy Cool.
They visit him and say,
"Please stop them mining on our land.
Please make them go away."

13

What can we do, thought Teddy Cool.
We all need soap to wash.
But digging up the countryside
Makes everybody cross.

I need a plan that works for all,
On which we can agree;
A plan that's fair for everyone,
The mine, my friends, and me.

First, we'll all stop buying soap.
That's sure to make some news.
Next, we'll write in to the press,
And let them know our views.

16

Then, I'll write a protest song
Which tells them what we think.
We'll sing and shout and dance about.
We'll kick up such a stink.

17

Off rode Teddy Cool to town,
To a big skyscraper tower.
He went to see the bosses there,
The ones with all the power.

18

In an office on the thirteenth floor,
Teddy Cool met three big chiefs.
He told them how their ugly mine
Was causing lots of grief.

19

"We must have soap to clean our bods,"
One chief said loud and strong.
"Without the soap to wash ourselves,
Imagine all the pong."

20

"The miners need to work for pay.
That's how they earn their money.
They need the work to buy their food,"
Said Ms. Betina Bunny.

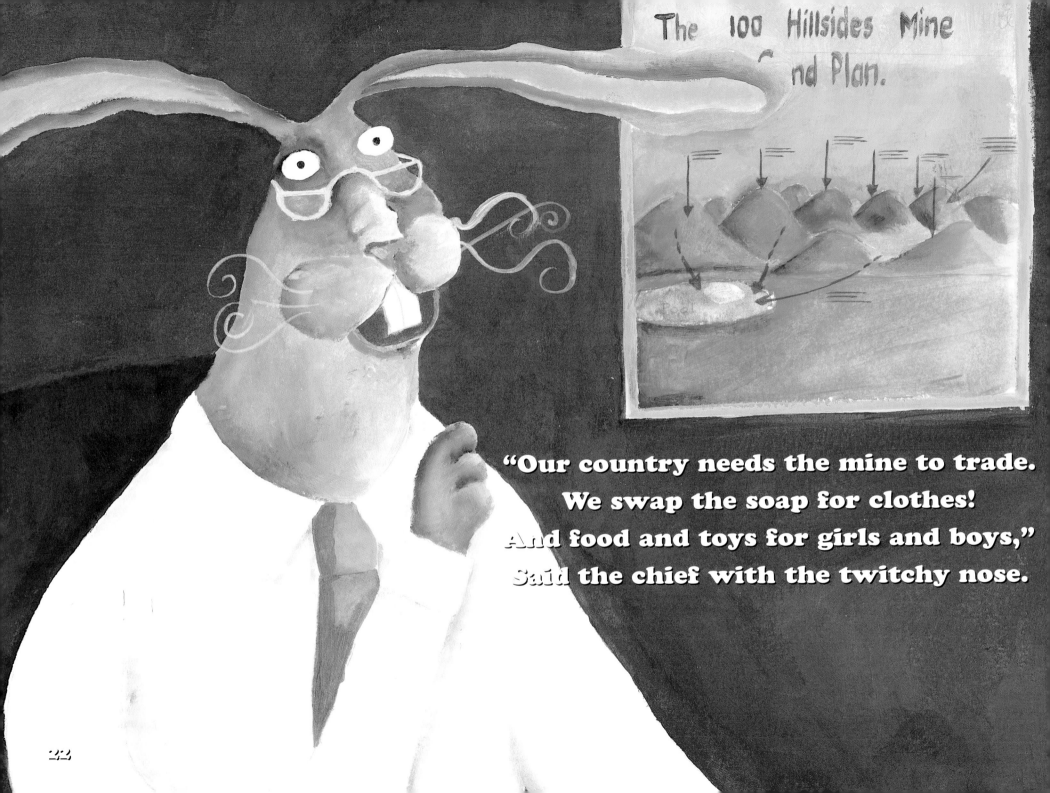

"Our country needs the mine to trade.
We swap the soap for clothes!
And food and toys for girls and boys,"
Said the chief with the twitchy nose.

"That may be so," said Teddy Cool.
"There's another reason too!
The soap mine makes a lot of cash,
For every one of you."

"You can't just take, you have to give.
It's wrong to just move in;
To dig up hills and cut down trees
And make a nasty din."

24

The faces of the chiefs went red.
Their embarrassment was funny.
But Ted stayed cool and calmly said,
"All you care about is money."

"Your soap mine spoils our lovely land.
It's noisy day and night!
Can I suggest to stop unrest,
You hide it out of sight."

"Use the muddy waste to build
New hills around the holes.
Then bring in trees with lots of leaves
To hide your planks and poles."

"And tell your trucks to take the road
That runs behind the mill.
The way they rattle, smoke and shake,
It makes us feel quite ill."

"When you do that, I promise this:
    We'll stop the angry letters.
    We'll all start using soap again.
    Don't you think that's better?"

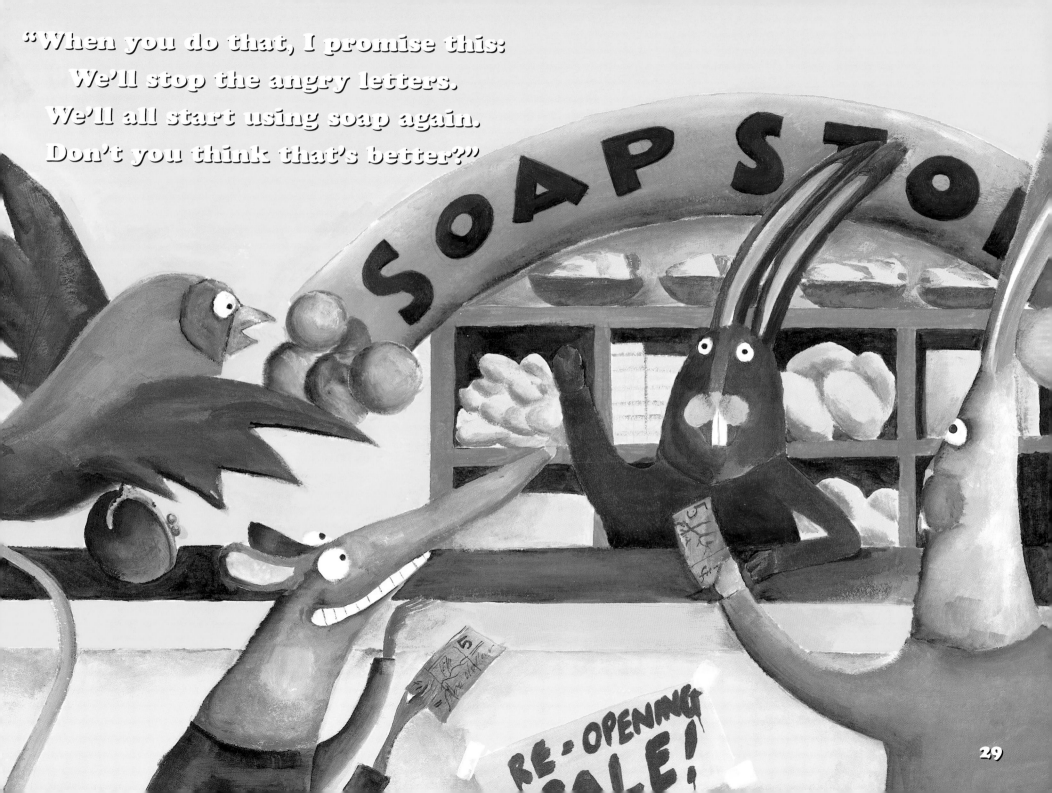

Happily, it all worked out.
The mine's now out of sight.
With no more trucks upon the road,
The future's looking bright.

And Teddy Cool's a happy bear.
His latest task is done.
So he'll do now what he does best,
That's having lots of fun.

The stream runs free of foam again.
The pool is clear once more.
And the Land of One Hundred Hillsides
Is now the Land of . . .

One Hundred and Four.